Maxwell Mutt
and The Biscuit & Bone Club

Also by Steve Voake:

Maxwell Mutt and the Downtown Dogs
Maxwell Mutt and the Squirrel Without A Story

Daisy Dawson
Daisy Dawson and the Secret Pool
Daisy Dawson and the Big Freeze
Daisy Dawson at the Seaside
Daisy Dawson on the Farm

Hooey Higgins and the Shark
Hooey Higgins and the Tremendous Trousers
Hooey Higgins and the Big Boat Race
Hooey Higgins Goes for Gold
Hooey Higgins and the Big Day Out
Hooey Higgins and the Awards of Awesomeness
Hooey Higgins and the Storm
Hooey Higgins and the Christmas Crash

Maxwell Mutt

and The Biscuit & Bone Club

Steve Voake

COVER ILLUSTRATION BY
Jim Field

INTERIOR ILLUSTRATIONS BY
Maxine Lee

WALKER
BOOKS

This is a work ~~of fiction. Names, characters, places and events~~ are either the product of the author's imagination or, if real, used fictitiously. All statements, activities, stunts, descriptions, information and material of any other kind contained herein are included for entertainment purposes only and should not be relied on for accuracy or replicated, as they may result in injury.

First published 2019 by Walker Books Ltd
87 Vauxhall Walk, London SE11 5HJ

2 4 6 8 10 9 7 5 3 1

Text © 2019 Steve Voake
Cover illustration © 2019 Jim Field
Interior illustrations © 2019 Maxine Lee

The right of Steve Voake, Jim Field and Maxine Lee to be identified as author and illustrators respectively of this work has been asserted by them in accordance with the Copyright, Designs and Patents Act 1988

This book has been typeset in Goudy Educational

Printed and bound in Great Britain
by CPI Group (UK) Ltd, Croydon CR0 4YY

British Library Cataloguing in Publication Data:
a catalogue record for this book is available from the British Library

ISBN 978-1-4063-5755-4

www.walker.co.uk

For my mum

S.V.

For my amazing friend, Meshelle

M.L.

CHAPTER ONE
Madison Gets a Job

"**FOUND YOU!**" said Maxwell. "Again."

Mr B sighed, took the bin lid from his head and came out from behind the dustbin. "I thought Hide and Seek was supposed to take longer than that."

"Maybe we need better places to hide," said Maxwell.

"Maybe we need more players," replied Mr B. "You know what they say: the more the merrier."

As he disappeared into the flowerbed, Maxwell heard a furious clucking sound and three chickens came pecking up the road, their wings all a-flutter.

"The farmer says to dance like nobody's watching," squawked one.

"But we *were* watching," replied another. "We'll show him there's more to chickens than just laying eggs."

"**DANCE, SQUAWK, REPEAT,**" clucked the

third. "**LET'S MOVE THOSE DANCIN' FEET...**"

"Hello," said Maxwell, popping his head through the gate. "Fancy a game of Hide and Seek?"

"Sorry, dogster, can't stop," replied the first chicken. "We're off to do some outdoor dancing."

Then, with a squawk and a flutter, the chickens strutted off.

"How odd," said Maxwell.

"Talking of odd," continued Mr B, emerging from the flowerbeds with a rose in his mouth, "where's Madison? He's supposed to be helping me pick out some new flowers for my kennel."

Maxwell frowned. "Madison said he'd help you with that?"

Mr B dropped the rose on the path next to a pile of dandelions. "He's working on his caring side—"

"**I HATE FOXES!** I want every last one of 'em gone!" yelled a red-faced man in riding boots as he suddenly barged past them.

Five foxhounds ran round the corner after him. "**YEAH!** Let's get 'em!" they barked.

"That's weird," said Mr B.

"I know," said Maxwell. "And you just missed three chickens passing by on their way to do outdoor dancing! Something strange is going on. It's all a bit of a mystery."

"Did someone say **MYSTERY**?" asked Restreppo, sticking his head around the corner. He was an ex-police dog and there was nothing he liked more than a mystery to solve.

"We've just seen a man running up the road shouting 'I hate foxes'," explained Mr B.

"That's not a mystery," said Restreppo. "That'll be the farmer fox-hunting with his hounds. Madison told me about them. He saw them at his new job out of town."

"Madison has a *job?*" Mr B's mouth fell open and he pushed it shut with his paw. "What kind of job?"

"It's at that new place in the woods," said Restreppo. "**The Biscuit and Bone Club.**"

"What's he doing there?"

"He's in charge of welcoming guests and making them feel at home. The spaniel from number seven reckons it might help with his anger issues. Plus he gets free biscuits."

"Free biscuits?" Mr B's eyes widened. "We can play Hide and Seek another day. Let's go see Madison at work!"

The three friends scampered to the back gate and followed the narrow lane behind the houses until they came to a field of sheep.

"Morning, ladies," called Mr B. "Lovely day."

"**DON'T BE CHASING US!**" cried the nearest sheep, nudging her lambs away. "There be laws 'bout chasing!"

"Don't worry," Maxwell reassured her. "We're just going to see our friend."

"Those bad hounds were chasing us!" said the mother sheep.

"**APPLE CHEEK TWIRLY-TOES,**" bleated a lamb. "**DANCEY FEET WELLY MAN.**"

Mr B frowned. "Are you talking about the farmer and his foxhounds?"

The lamb nodded.

"Why do you call him that?"

"Because he dances round the field when he thinks no one's looking," replied the ewe.

"Hmm," said Restreppo. "Three chickens and a farmer who likes to dance. The plot thickens."

The sheep stared at him blankly.

"He used to be a police dog," explained Mr B.

The ewe tugged on a mouthful of grass. "**I LOVE GRASS**," she said.

"Have you seen our friend Madison?" Maxwell asked. "He's got big hair and shouts a lot."

The sheep thought for a moment, then nodded. "I saw him today. He was arguing with Ramsey, and Ramsey said: 'Seems like you've got a temper on you, son.' And your friend said, 'That's why I'm going up **The Biscuit and Bone Club**.' Then Ramsey ate some more grass. I love grass, I do."

"Grass is lush," agreed another sheep. "So green and juicy."

Mr B sighed. "You don't get out much, do you?"

"We're always out," said the sheep.

"Do you remember which way Madison went?" asked Maxwell.

"Scampered up the hill," said the ewe, pulling up more grass. "I love grass, I do. It tastes so—"

"OK, great," said Mr B. "Thanks for your help. Come on guys – this way!"

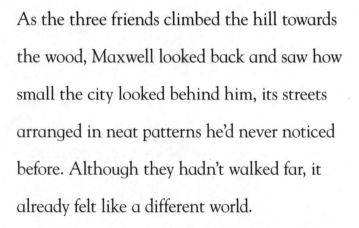

CHAPTER TWO
iNTO The WoodS

As the three friends climbed the hill towards the wood, Maxwell looked back and saw how small the city looked behind him, its streets arranged in neat patterns he'd never noticed before. Although they hadn't walked far, it already felt like a different world.

The sun shone from a clear blue sky and Maxwell's special listening gift meant he could hear not only the bleat of lambs and the fumble of bees, but also the patter of mice and the singing of moles beneath the earth. As the three dogs entered the wood, the sounds grew fainter until all he could hear was the wind in the trees.

"Are you sure this is the way to the club?" asked Mr B. "I haven't seen any signs."

"It's an animal club, not a human club," said Restreppo. "That's why it's hard to find. But if Madison found it, so can we."

The wood was bigger than Maxwell had imagined. Although it was a summer's day, the trees were so close together they almost shut out the sky and the forest grew deep and dark. As the gaps between the trees became

narrower, Maxwell realized that any human
travellers would be unlikely to pass this way.

"These greens and browns are very
relaxing," said Mr B. "I can feel my stress just
draining away."

"Oh, because your life's *SO* stressful," said
Restreppo. "Ooh, shall I lie on this lilac

cushion? Or on that sherbert-lemon one?"

"My stress," replied Mr B, "comes from living next door to a sarcastic Alsatian."

"Mr B's right, though," said Maxwell, keen to avoid an argument. "Green *is* a relaxing colour."

"Officer Marshall took me running in these fields the other day," said Restreppo. "We saw a river, with a big round wooden thing in it. Officer Marshall said it was a water wheel."

"How fascinating," said Mr B.

"Now who's being sarcastic?"

"**SHUSH**, you two!" said Maxwell. He lifted an ear and listened. "Did you hear that?"

"Probably Mr B's stomach," said Restreppo.

Mr B nodded. "I've been cutting out carbs. They play havoc with my digestion."

"No, it's not that," said Maxwell. He listened again and heard the faint chatter of squirrels, the squeak of a mouse and the growl of a cross poodle. "I think I hear Madison," he said.

Squeezing through a patch of brambles, the three dogs stumbled out into a clearing where dappled sunlight danced across the grass. In front of them was a shelter built of branches, tied together with lengths of vine pulled from the trees. A piece of wood had been nailed above the door and scratched onto it was a picture of a dog biscuit next to a bone. Laughter floated through the open door.

"Look!" said Restreppo. "A biscuit and a bone! This could be **The Biscuit and Bone Club**!"

"Wow," said Mr B. "Can't think why you never made detective."

At that moment, Madison appeared in the doorway. "**WHAT ARE YOU LOT DOING HERE?**" he scowled.

"I thought you were supposed to be a welcomer," said Mr B. "I don't feel in the least bit special."

"Oh, you're something special all right," said Madison.

Mr B turned to the others. "Is he being rude? I think he's being rude."

24

"OK, *fine*," said Madison, gritting his teeth. "Welcome to **The Biscuit and Bone Club**. A brand new club open to all animals regardless of breed, colour or…" here he looked at Mr B "…intelligence."

"You're so funny, Madison," said Mr B. "How's the anger management coming along, by the way?"

Madison growled, then took a deep breath, pressed his paws together and said, "How utterly lovely to see you all. Please, if you would: follow me."

"*Whatever they're feeding him,*" whispered Mr B, "*we need a lifetime's supply.*"

Then the three dogs stepped out of the heat and into the cool shadows of the club.

CHAPTER THREE

The Biscuit & Bone Club

Sunlight streamed through old jam jars that had been set into the roof, lighting up clusters of animals gathered below them. Some sat on upturned logs, some huddled on hummocks of heather, while others leaned against the walls of the clubhouse. Everyone was talking, laughing and drinking from tiny bowls. In one corner, two rats listened to a group of

mice discussing cheese while a company of
moles swapped tunnel stories over a plate of
worms. Three squirrels were discussing the
weather with a grass snake called Nigel.

"I don't know about you, Nige," said one
squirrel, "but when it's really hot I have, like,
zero energy."

"That's me in a nutshell," agreed another.

"See, now I don't mind the heat," said

Nigel. "Stick me on a stone and I'll cook 'til the cows come home. But running around in the treetops? Forget it."

"Forget it!" laughed the squirrels, pushing a bowl of water in the snake's direction. "There y'go, Nige. Get your forked tongue round that."

"Cheersssss."

"This place is **AMAZiNG**," said Maxwell, taking it all in. "I wonder who runs it?"

"There's your answer," said Restreppo.

Maxwell turned to see two monkeys working behind the bar. One was wiping it down with a damp leaf while the other was setting out little plates of broken biscuits.

"Got any more bones?" asked an old foxhound who was standing at the bar, holding an empty bowl between his teeth.

"Sorry, Jake," said the first monkey, wringing out the leaf and hanging it up to dry, "you've had the last one. But the seagulls down by the butcher's are bringing up a fresh delivery in the morning."

"i DON'T BELiEVE iT!" exclaimed Maxwell, recognizing his two friends from the city zoo. "iT'S MEGAN AND MONTY!"

"Maxwell!" cried Megan, jumping over the bar. "Monty, look who's here!"

"Well I never," said Monty. "This calls for a celebration!" He brought out several bowls of fresh berry water, and Maxwell and his friends made themselves comfortable on a pile of bracken.

"Did you build all this yourself?" asked Maxwell.

Megan nodded. "After the rumpus at the zoo, we followed the squirrels over the wall and didn't look back. We built a place out here away from it all and opened it up to any animal who happened to be passing by."

"We never expected it to get this busy," said Monty. "But just look around you. Nobody's in a cage. No one cares what you look like or what kind of animal you are. Everyone's free to come and go as they please and everyone looks out for one another."

"When we were stuck in the zoo, I used to imagine a place like this," said Megan. "And now here we are."

"Living the dream," said Mr B.

"Dreams are all very well," growled old Jake the foxhound. "But sooner or later you have to wake up."

Mr B looked at him sideways. "Does anyone want to swap places?" he muttered.

At that moment there was a rustle of leaves and a vixen burst through the entrance and tumbled onto the floor. Picking herself up, she shook herself and looked around with wide fearful eyes.

"Please," she said, "you have to help me. The foxhounds are after my blood."

CHAPTER FOUR
Fox in Danger

"I don't understand," said Maxwell as he pushed a bowl of berry water towards the frightened fox. "Why would foxhounds want to hurt you?"

"Because the farmer hates me," she replied.

"Maybe you shouldn't have eaten his chickens," growled Jake from his position at the bar.

"I didn't," said the vixen. She took a sip

of berry water and glanced nervously at the scowling hound. "I only take the food that people have left in their bins. I need it to feed my cubs."

"A likely story," said Jake. "Anyway, the sooner you leave the better. We don't want your sort around here."

"But you heard what Megan said?" Maxwell reminded Jake. "Everyone is welcome here."

"I don't want any trouble," said the vixen. "Just as soon as I've caught my breath, I'll be on my way."

"Not before you've had something to eat, you won't," said Mr B, taking a plate of biscuits from the bar and setting it down in front of her.

"Maybe just a bite then," said the vixen. "My name's Fern, by the way."

"And I'm Maxwell," said Maxwell.

"Don't be getting too friendly," said Jake. "The hounds are on their way and if you've got any sense, you'll be gone before they get here. If I wasn't retired, I'd be chasing you myself."

Maxwell saw that Fern was trembling. But she was also watching Jake as he propped himself up against the bar.

"What have you done to your paw?" she asked.

"Nothing," said Jake, "if it's any business of yours."

"It doesn't look like nothing."

"Life hurts," replied Jake, "and you've just got to learn to live with it."

"Or you can try and make it better," suggested Fern. Then she turned and ran out of the door.

"See?" said Jake. "She's the same as the rest of them. Causing trouble and running scared."

But seconds later Fern reappeared with a bunch of purple flowers in her mouth. She trotted over to Jake and dropped the flowers in front of him. The other animals all stopped talking.

In the distance, Maxwell heard the barking of foxhounds. "Fern," he said, "they're coming this way. You have to go."

"Not yet," replied Fern. She turned back to

Jake. "Show me your paw."

"What? No."

"Come on. I won't hurt you."

Jake winced as Fern tugged at his paw.

When she turned it over, Maxwell saw it was

red and swollen.

"I cut it on some barbed wire," said Jake. "Guess I'm too old to be chasing foxes. But I miss it, you know? The thrill of the chase and all that."

"Maybe you need a hobby," said Mr B.

"Hold still," said Fern. She rolled the flowers together and pressed them onto Jake's swollen paw. "It's called Woundwort. I often use it for cuts and bruises. Soon your paw will be good as new."

Maxwell lifted one ear and heard the faint sound of a hunting horn. "Fern," he said, "how far is your home from here?"

"About a thousand breaths," she said. "I live by the circle in the river."

"The hounds are nearly here," said Maxwell. "If you go now, we'll try and keep them long enough for you to get home."

Megan pointed behind the bar. "You're safer going out the back way."

As Fern padded past Maxwell, she stopped and gave him a hug. "Thank you, Maxwell," she said. "You're a good friend."

Then she was gone.

Maxwell listened to the yaps and growls getting closer. Then a pack of snarling hounds burst through the front door, led by a fierce dog with wild, staring eyes.

She sniffed the air and looked around. "TRACKER, SNiFFER, CHECK THE BACK!" she barked. "SEEKER, STALKER, TAKE THE SiDES."

As the other hounds disappeared, their leader walked calmly towards the bar.

"Well, if it isn't old Jake," she said when she saw the old foxhound. "How's retirement?"

"Hello, Hunter," said Jake. "Retirement is quiet. Just the way I like it."

Hunter stared at him for a few moments, then turned to Megan. "**YOU**. Give me a bowl of your best berry water."

"*Please*," muttered Madison, who had followed them in.

Hunter glared at him.

"It's OK, Madison," said Megan. "Just be nice." She turned to Hunter. "Madison's been working on his **ANGER MANAGEMENT**.

He's doing really well, aren't you
Madison?"

Madison gritted his teeth and
nodded. "Welcome to **The Biscuit
and Bone Club**," he said. "How
may we be of service today?"

"Like I said," continued Hunter. "A bowl of
your best berry water and **MAKE iT SNAPPY.**"

Madison was about to say something else
when Maxwell nudged him. *"Fern needs time,"*
he whispered. *"We need to keep them talking."*

Hunter spun round and stared at Maxwell.
"WHAT DiD YOU SAY?"

Maxwell gulped. "I said the weather's fine.
Lovely day for walking."

"Hmm," said the foxhound, glancing around the bar. "I think you all know who I'm looking for."

"That special someone, maybe?" suggested Mr B. "Good sense of humour and a bubbly personality?"

"I'm looking for a fox," said Hunter. "A vixen, to be precise. With dark red fur and a splodge of white on her tail."

"Maybe you should lower your standards," said Mr B.

Hunter glared at him. "**ARE YOU TRYING TO BE FUNNY?**"

Mr B was about to make another joke when he saw the way Hunter was looking at him and stared at the floor.

"I'll ask again," growled Hunter. "Has anyone seen her?"

The mice hid behind the tables, the moles hid behind the squirrels and Nigel the snake noisily swallowed a biscuit.

The dogs all shook their heads.

"That's strange," said Hunter. "Do you want to know why?"

"*Not really*," whispered Mr B.

Hunter took a deep breath, then let it out again, long and slow. "Because," she said, "I can smell **FOX**."

CHAPTER FIVE
HuNTeR aNd The HouNds

Monty dropped the jam jar he had been
cleaning and it shattered on the floor. "OOPS,"
he said, sweeping the broken glass into a pile
with his foot. "I'm such a monkey-mitts!"

Hunter turned to look at Jake. "What
about you, old dog? Would you say a fox has
been this way?"

Jake nodded. "As a matter of fact I would."

The other animals gasped.

"I thought as much," said Hunter. She smiled, showing a mouthful of cracked yellow teeth. "So, where is she?"

"Last time I saw her she was heading north up into the woods," replied Jake. He shifted his paw and winced. "But she was moving pretty fast. If you want to catch her, you should probably get going."

Hunter frowned. "You'd better not be telling stories."

"If it's stories you're after, I've got a head full of 'em," replied Jake. "But all the time we're talking, there's a fox who's getting further away."

Hunter studied him for a few moments. Then she barked, "OK, everyone, let's move out!" The rest of the pack skidded past the bar and followed her out of the door. As they disappeared into the trees, their yelps became fainter and fainter until at last only Maxwell could hear them.

"I can't believe it," said Mr B, staring at Jake. "After Fern helped you with your paw and everything! How could you?"

"He didn't," said Maxwell. "He sent them the wrong way."

Restreppo frowned. "How do you know?"

"Fern said she lived by a circle in the river – and the river is down in the valley. But Jake sent the hounds up the hill."

Jake nodded. "Maxwell's a smart pup," he said. "But those hounds aren't stupid. Pretty soon they're going to figure out I sent them in the wrong direction. And when they do, they'll do what they're best at."

"And what's that?" asked Restreppo.

"Hunting foxes," said Jake. He thought for a moment. "Does anyone know where this river circle is?"

"I saw it when I went out with Officer Marshall," said Restreppo. "The sun was shining on the water and there was a big wooden circle turning around in the river."

Ridley Rat put his paw in the air. "I know where that is," he said.

"It's the water mill down in the valley, just below Sunset Hill."

"Then we need to be quick," said Maxwell. "Restreppo, you and Madison are the fastest, so you can head over to Fern's place and make sure she gets there safely. Mr B and I will try to lead the hounds in the opposite direction."

"**EH?**" said Mr B. "How will we do that?"

"Don't worry," said Maxwell, "I'll explain on the way!"

CHAPTER SIX

MAXWELL'S PLAN

"**I DON'T GET IT,**" said Mr B as he and Maxwell scampered back into the woods. "Why would the hounds follow us?"

"Because of the scent," replied Maxwell. "Before she left, Fern hugged me, remember? We're closer to the hounds than she is, so when they realize they've been tricked they'll pick up her scent on me and track *us*, thinking they're following *her*."

Mr B frowned. "You really think that will work?"

"There's only one way to find out."

"But Jake's a foxhound too," said Mr B. "Why didn't he give her away? Why didn't he tell them where she'd gone?"

"Because she helped him," said Maxwell. "He wasn't the same dog after that."

"And we won't be the same if those hounds catch us," said Mr B. "Did you SEE the size of their teeth?"

"If we're going to save Fern," replied Maxwell, "that's a risk we have to take."

He stopped and lifted one ear.

"What is it?" asked Mr B.

"The hounds are on the move again," said Maxwell. "They're coming this way."

As the pair hurried through the woods, the trees thinned out and the sun grew stronger. The air smelled of fresh leaves and warm wood; wild garlic flowers blossomed in dappled sunlight, their star-shaped petals shining in a sea of green. Maxwell slid down a moss-covered slope and into a gully of ferns, their feathery leaves tickling his ears as he tumbled beneath the trees.

"I could do with something to drink," panted Mr B. "**I'M HEATING UP LIKE A HOT DOG.**"

Maxwell stopped and listened again. In the distance he could hear the splash and bubble of water over stones.

"Follow me," he said and set off through the trees.

After a while they reached a sparkling

stream, twisting and tumbling towards the valley below.

With a yelp, Mr B leapt straight in, and Maxwell scampered after him, the water cool against his hot, aching paws.

"HEY, MAXWELL, LOOK!" called Mr B when he had finished drinking. "A WATERFALL!"

Maxwell waded downstream and stood next to his friend, watching the glittering water tumble into the deep pool below.

"What do you reckon?" asked Mr B.

"FANCY A SWIM?"

"I'm not sure," said Maxwell. "Do we have time?"

"Hmm, let me think," said Mr B. Then he leapt over the edge and hit the surface of the pool so hard that a plume of spray shot high into the air. When Maxwell peered over the edge all he could see was a stream of silver bubbles rising to the surface.

"MR B," he called. "ARE YOU ALL RIGHT?"

For a moment the world was silent.

Then Mr B's head broke through the
surface and he cupped his paws around his
mouth, shouting, "**COME ON, MAXWELL – THE
WATER'S WONDERFUL!**"

Maxwell had never wanted anything quite
so much as to leap down into the deep, cool
waterfall pool. But as he was about to jump,
he heard the distant sound of barking and
remembered why they had come.

"**HURRY UP!**" called Mr B. "What are you
waiting for?"

Maxwell looked longingly down at the
pool and shook his head. "I can't," he said,
stepping firmly back from the edge.

When Mr B found him, he was sitting in the shade of an old beech tree. "Why didn't you come in?" he asked.

"The water would have washed Fern's scent away," said Maxwell. "I couldn't risk it."

Mr B patted him gently. "You have a good heart," he said. "And a hot head."

"I've been thinking about that water wheel," said Maxwell. "Ridley said it was by Sunset Hill. So if the sun sets over where Fern lives, then we need to be heading in the opposite direction."

He looked up and saw that dark clouds were gathering overhead.

"That doesn't look good," he said. "I'm

starting to get a **BAD FEELiNG** about this."

"No need for bad feelings, young pup!" squawked a voice from nowhere.

Then three chickens burst out of the undergrowth, flung their wings wide and chorused:

"TAH-DAH!"

CHAPTER SEVEN

The Checkout Chickens

Maxwell and Mr B stared in disbelief as the

chickens squawked:

"One, two, three, four..."

and started to dance and sing:

"When you're sad and feeling beat
When you're melting in the heat

All you gotta do is move your feet
And just dance, dance, dance!"

"OOH, i LOVE iT," said Mr B, standing up on his hind legs and swaying his hips. "MOVE iT, MAXWELL!"

And before Maxwell knew what was happening, the chickens fluttered around him and he was dancing too.

"When you're staring at defeat
When your life's no longer sweet
All you gotta do is move your feet
C'mon dance, dance, dance!"

"BREAK iT DOWN!"

squawked a chicken,
and the trio shimmied
from side to side, their
beaks in the air.

"Hum-diddy dum-diddy dum-dum-dum
Rum-tiddy dum-tiddy rum-tum-tum
Hum-diddy dum-diddy dum-dum-dum
So let's dance, dance, dance ... hoy!"

They froze in their positions for a moment, then broke out of formation to congratulate Mr B and Maxwell on their dance moves.

"You were *so* in time," said one.

"You two are naturals," said another.

"Do you really think so?" asked Mr B.

"Absolutely," said a third. "With a bit more practice you could join us **CHECKOUT CHICKENS!**"

Maxwell frowned. "Why are you called that?"

"Because we dug ourselves a tunnel and now we can **CHECK OUT** of the chicken run whenever we like. I'm **CHERRY**, that's **CHIQUITA** and this is **CHELSEA**."

"**HOW Y'DOiN'**," said Chelsea, waving a wing. "Pleased to meet you."

"Likewise," laughed Maxwell. "I didn't know chickens could dance."

"We taught ourselves," Cherry explained. "It all started when we saw the farmer doing this cute dance around the yard when he thought no one was watching. And we thought, *Hey, we could do that! Let's show him we're not all about the eggs, girls!*"

"The farmer was *dancing?*" asked Maxwell, remembering that the sheep had said the same thing.

"He dances a *lot*," said Chiquita. "He stands outside the chicken run and lifts his arms in the air like this…" she waved her wings gently up and down "…just like a birdy."

"We've worked out a few moves of our own since then," said Chelsea, "but the birdy one's our favourite, isn't it, girls?"

Cherry nodded. "Which is why we've come out here to rehearse. So we can show that old farmer how it's *really* done."

Maxwell thought about the dancing farmer who hated foxes. Life was full of surprises.

Then, in the distance, he heard the rumble of thunder and the barking of dogs.

"The hounds are moving away," he said. "I think they might be losing the scent."

"What do you mean?" asked Cherry.

"Maxwell can hear the foxhounds," explained Mr B. "It's a long story, but basically we're trying to get them to chase us."

The chickens gasped. "Are you **FOXES**?"

"Do we *look* like foxes?" said Mr B.

"Dunno," said Chiquita. "Never seen one."

At that moment there was a flash of lightning and the rain came roaring through the branches.

"**HELP!**" squawked the chickens. "**THE SKY iS FALLiNG ON OUR HEADS!**"

The animals tried to run for cover, but the rain was so heavy that it ripped through the leaves and churned up the forest floor, flooding the gullies and soaking Maxwell's fur. Water dripped from the end of his nose and his paws squelched as he walked.

"**SPLiSH!**" said Cherry.

"**SPLASH!**" added Chiquita.

"**SPLOSH!**" agreed Chelsea.

71

"**WHERE ARE WE GOING?**" shouted Mr B as they stumbled through the trees, but his words were lost in the wind.

The sky was dark: Maxwell watched the water run over his paws and shook his head. "I can't hear the hounds any more. They must have found Fern's real scent and gone after her."

He couldn't help remembering how happy everyone had been at **The Biscuit and Bone Club**, all the animals laughing and joking and drinking their berry water. It didn't seem fair that Fern's life was in danger just because the farmer didn't like her.

But what could a small dog do against an angry farmer and a fierce pack of hounds?

As the bedraggled little group carried on walking, Maxwell realized that it had stopped raining and the sun had come out. All around them the ground steamed in the sunlight. He looked through the trees and saw blue sky again; they had reached the edge of the wood. They were halfway up a hill, which sloped down to a field of golden corn.

"That is quite a view," said Mr B.

A warm wind rippled through the corn like a wave. In the distance, the river sparkled beneath Sunset Hill.

"There's the mill!" barked Mr B, pointing at a tiny wheel turning slowly in the distance.

"The circle in the water," said Maxwell
thoughtfully.

He watched two tiny dots running towards
it and realized he was looking at Restreppo
and Madison.

"The hounds are above us," he said, lifting
his ears. "They're about to come out at the
edge of the wood."

"Is that bad?" asked Mr B.

Maxwell nodded. "They'll see where Madison and Restreppo are heading and guess that's where Fern lives. Unless…"

"Unless what?" asked the bulldog.

"Unless we can create a diversion," replied Maxwell. He turned to the chickens. "Cherry, Chelsea, Chiquita?"

The chickens, who were busy stomping their feet and shaking raindrops from their feathers, stopped and looked at him expectantly.

"We know you're good at dancing, but how good are you at clucking and squawking and running away?"

Chiquita looked Maxwell squarely in the eye. "Those things," she said, "are the things we do best."

"In that case," said Maxwell, "I have a plan. But I'm going to need your help."

Chiquita nodded solemnly. "**THE CHECKOUT CHICKENS,**" she said, "**ARE AT YOUR SERVICE.**"

CHAPTER EIGHT

Through the Cornfield

Breaking out of their planning huddle, the three chickens looked both ways, then sneaked down the hill and hid behind a gorse bush.

"So far so good," said Maxwell, then lay down and started rolling around in the mud. Mr B returned with some berries and began squashing them into his friend's fur until it turned a reddish, muddy brown.

"What do you think?" asked Maxwell. "Do

I look anything like a fox?"

"Not from here," admitted Mr B. "But with any luck, they'll be far enough away for you to be in with a chance."

Maxwell sat up and listened. "They're nearly at the tree line," he said.

The two dogs ran back to the edge of the wood. When they had taken up their positions, Maxwell signalled to the chickens.

"Ready?" he called.

The chickens rose up from the gorse bush and raised their wings in unison.

"OK," said Maxwell. "**WISH ME LUCK.**"

As he raced down the slope the chickens broke cover, squawking and flapping their wings and running away from him, down the hill towards the cornfield. Glancing over his shoulder, Maxwell saw Hunter and the hounds appear from the trees and hoped that, from a distance, he looked like a fox chasing after chickens. His heart thumping, he scrambled down to the bottom of the hill and plunged into the field, stalks of corn flattening in front of him.

"EVERYONE SPLiT UP!" squawked Chiquita, and the chickens flapped off into the cornfield. The sun was hot and Maxwell could feel the mud drying and cracking on his back, flakes of it falling as his paws thumped across the ground.

Behind him the tails of the hounds swished through the corn, their grunts and snarls getting closer with every step.

What would they do when they caught up with him?

Maxwell ran faster and faster. Stalks of corn whipped against his face and he gasped for breath. He was just beginning to wonder if he would ever make it to the other side when he stumbled out of the field and collapsed onto the riverbank. Suddenly four foxhounds surrounded him, blocking out the sun.

"SO, YOU THOUGHT YOU COULD OUTRUN US, DID YOU?" barked a familiar voice. "Thought you could beat us down to the river?"

Maxwell opened one eye and saw Hunter silhouetted against the light, flanked by the rest of her pack, teeth bared and drooling.

"I guessed you'd catch up with me in the end," Maxwell said. "But I know you like a chase, so I thought I'd give you a proper run out."

"How very thoughtful," snarled Hunter.

Maxwell wondered when the hounds would guess he wasn't a real fox. He shivered.

"OK, son," said Hunter. "Move out of the way now. Me and the boys have some business to attend to."

"Well, I guess you got your fox in the end," said Maxwell bravely.

To Maxwell's surprise, Hunter began to laugh. "Did you hear that, boys? **THE KID THINKS HE'S A FOX.**"

The other hounds chuckled unpleasantly.

"**WHY, HELLO, LITTLE FOX**," said one. "Did you have fun chasing all those chickens?"

"But I *am* a fox," said Maxwell. "Can't you see?"

"I can see you're covered in mud and berry juice," said Hunter. "But that doesn't make you a fox any more than running through a cornfield makes me a loaf of bread."

The other hounds sniggered.

But as Hunter stepped closer, Maxwell saw that she had stopped laughing. "**WAIT. IS THAT WHAT YOU THINK?** You think we followed you down here because we saw you chasing chickens and mistook you for *a fox*?"

Maxwell stared at the ground and said nothing.

"The reason we followed you down here," said Hunter, "is that we guessed you were coming to warn your little foxy friend. I'm right, aren't I?"

Maxwell's heart beat faster until he remembered what Fern had said about living by the circle in the water. With any luck she'd be safely at the water mill by now. "If that's what you think," he said, "why don't you go ahead and look?"

"Oh, don't worry," said Hunter. "We will."

Maxwell followed Hunter's gaze to the far side of the river. A clump of willows dipped their branches in the water and, in the shadows beneath, Maxwell saw a pair of eyes staring back at him from a hole in the river bank. It was only when he turned to look at the stone bridge and saw its semi-circular arch of bricks reflected in the water that he realized his mistake.

The circle in the river!

Fern didn't live by the water mill at all. She lived here, by the bridge. By trying to help her, Maxwell had simply made things worse.

He had led the foxhounds straight to her home.

CHAPTER NINE

Saving Fern

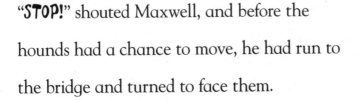

"**STOP!**" shouted Maxwell, and before the hounds had a chance to move, he had run to the bridge and turned to face them.

"**MOVE AWAY!**" commanded Hunter.

Maxwell's legs trembled, but he stood his ground and shook his head. "I'm not going anywhere."

"Then you are protecting a fox," said Hunter. "And if you are protecting a fox, we will treat you like one. Do you understand?"

Maxwell understood only too well. But Fern and her cubs were in danger. He took a deep breath, clenched his paws and looked Hunter squarely in the eye. "Like I said, I'm not going anywhere."

"**DON'T BE A FOOL**," growled Hunter. "**MOVE OUT OF MY WAY.**"

"It's me you want," said a soft voice.

Maxwell turned to see Fern standing behind

him, her red fur shining in the sun. She calmly padded over and sat down. "If I stay, I want you to promise you'll leave my friend alone."

"i DON'T BARGAiN WiTH FOXES," snapped the hound, the pack panting and snarling behind her.

Fern turned to Maxwell. "You've done all you can," she said. "Now you must save yourself."

Maxwell thought about all the good things in his life: his friends, the pool in the woods, his comfortable kennel back home. He looked at the slavering dogs, and just for a moment he was tempted to run. But he knew deep down that he would never leave Fern to face the hounds alone.

"**NO**," he said. "I'm staying here with you." Then, as Hunter leapt forward, Maxwell threw himself sideways and knocked Fern off the bridge. "**SWiM!**" he barked. "**SWiM! SWiM!**"

Jumping over Hunter, Maxwell ducked through the legs of the rest of the hounds and plunged back into the corn. The dogs charged after him, barking and howling.

Maxwell raced desperately through the tangle of stems, doubled back and emerged once more beside the river.

"**FERN!**" he called, running along the riverbank and searching for signs of life in the water. "**FERN! WHERE ARE YOU?**"

But the only sound was the yelping of hounds coming through the corn towards him.

Exhausted, Maxwell collapsed on the muddy bank and waited for them to arrive.

"WHAT WERE YOU THINKING?" barked
Hunter, crashing out of the cornfield followed
by the rest of the pack. "Why did you push
her in the river?"

"I was trying to save her," replied Maxwell.

"That worked out well, then," said one of
the other hounds.

"Oh, come on, cheer up," said Hunter.
"Everyone knows that foxes are bad news,
chasing chickens and frightening them away."

"But Fern *didn't* chase the chickens!" replied
Maxwell. "The chickens left the farm because
they wanted to practise their dance to show
the farmer later!"

"You expect me to believe that?"

asked Hunter.

"It's true, whether you believe it or not."

"**WHATEVER,**" said Hunter. "If the farmer says foxes are bad news, that's good enough for me."

In the distance, Maxwell heard the sound of a hunting horn and a galloping horse. A few moments later the hounds pricked up their ears and began jumping up and down.

"**THE FARMER! THE FARMER!**" they barked. "**HERE COMES THE FARMER!**"

A chestnut stallion swished through the corn and galloped to a halt, the red-faced farmer on its back.

"**HURRAH FOR MY HOUNDS!**" he bellowed.

"Finally cornered that wily fox, have you?" He raised the hunting horn to his lips and blew as hard as he could. *Ta-ran-ta-rah!* "Right, let's see what you've done with her!"

"Well, this is embarrassing," said one of the hounds.

"Come on, where is she?" demanded the farmer, looking sternly at the pack.

Hunter glared at Maxwell. "This is all your fault."

"I know," said Maxwell.

At that moment he heard a soft splash and noticed the water rippling beneath the willows. From the corner of his eye he saw Fern swimming in the shadows on the far side of the river. So far he seemed to be the only one who had seen her. She was alive! His heart leapt with joy, but he had to take care that he didn't give her away.

Please, he willed her as she paddled silently across to the far bank. *Don't make a sound.*

"I'm sorry to have caused you all this trouble," he said to Hunter, deliberately not looking in Fern's direction, "but as the fox has gone, I suppose we might as well all go home."

The hounds grumbled and turned back towards the cornfield.

"Ah, picked up her scent again, have you?" grunted the farmer. "Go on, then."

Maxwell glanced back to see Fern standing silently in the shallows. He breathed a sigh of relief. In a moment the farmer and his hounds would be gone and Fern would be safely home.

But suddenly there was a flutter of wings, a squawk of **"YEEE-ESSS!"**, and three chickens

flapped their way towards the bridge. As
Maxwell watched in horror, Cherry, Chiquita
and Chelsea slipped and slid their way down
to the little stony beach where Fern was
shaking the water from her fur.

"**HEY!**" yelled the farmer, jumping down
from his horse. "Those are my missing
chickens! And look! Down by the river! It's
that blasted fox!"

With a furious bark, Hunter bounded back out of the corn. **"GET THAT FOX!"** she howled.

But as the hounds began to run across the bridge the farmer shouted, **"WAiT!"** and Hunter stopped so suddenly that the other hounds piled into the back of her, tumbling over in a cloud of dust.

For a moment, there was an eerie silence. Then, as the dust settled, Maxwell saw that the chickens had stepped in front of Fern and were waving the hounds back across the bridge with their wings.

"Stop your nonsense and pay attention!" squawked Chiquita.

"Are you ready for the **BiG SHOW**?" called Chelsea.

"Presenting ...

the ...

Check ...

Out ...

CHICKENS!"

clucked Cherry.

The farmer and his hounds stared open-mouthed as the chickens closed their eyes and began dancing lightly on the tips of their scrawny feet, moving their wings gracefully up and down.

"It *can't* be!" whispered the farmer, so softly

that only Maxwell could hear. "That's the

dance from *Swan Lake*!"

As the chickens floated elegantly across

the stony beach, the corn rustled and Mr B

appeared beside Maxwell. "How did it go?" he

asked breathlessly. "Did you fool them?"

He stopped and stared at the hounds before following their gaze across the river to the dancing chickens.

"OK, THAT'S WEIRD. Does anyone else think that's weird?"

"It *is* weird," agreed the horse. "They're doing the farmer's dance. The one he practises every night when he thinks no one's looking."

"Apparently it's called *Swan Lake*," said Maxwell.

"**CHiCKEN LAKE** more like," said Mr B, at which point the farmer gave a little cry and clasped his hands to his chest.

"*Such beauty*," he whispered. "*Such a vision of feathered loveliness.*"

The hounds looked sideways at each other. One coughed awkwardly while another gazed at the ground and a third tried to remember where he'd buried his bone.

The farmer wiped away a tear with the back of his hand. Then to everyone's surprise, he ran down the riverbank, jumped into the water and waded across to the other side.

"Well, hit me over the head with a hay bale," said the horse.

"Here he comes," squawked Chelsea as the farmer clambered onto the bank. "Get ready to take a bow."

"Please," said the farmer. "Don't stop."

And then, he began to dance too.

"**CHECK THAT OUT**," said the horse as the farmer tottered around the chickens on tiptoes, flapping his arms up and down. "Just when you think you've seen it all."

"What's happening?" barked Restreppo, stumbling out of the cornfield closely followed by Madison.

Mr B shushed him and nodded across the water.

"**A BALLET-DANCING FARMER**," said Madison. "I did not see that coming."

The chickens formed a circle and as the farmer pirouetted into the centre they sang:

"Dum dumdy-dumdy-dum dee-dum,
Dee-dum dee-dumdy-dumdy-dum"

They sang so slowly and mournfully that the hounds threw back their heads and howled.

"Oh dear, I think I've got something in my eye," said Mr B, pressing his paws against his face.

"Go ahead," said a foxhound, patting him on the back. "**LET iT ALL OUT.**"

"Dum dumdy-dumdy-dum dee-dum,
Dee-dum dee-dumdy-dumdy-dum"

sang the chickens, and gradually the farmer

bent his knees and danced lower and lower

until, with a final flourish, he collapsed on

the ground like a dying swan.

"**BRAVO!**" cried the horse. "**ENCORE!**"

"I can't cope!" sobbed Mr B. "It's so moving!"

The hounds hollered, the chickens cheered
and only Maxwell noticed Fern edging

slowly away from the
riverbank with her
cubs by her side.
Just for a moment,
she stopped and
looked at Maxwell.
Then with a twitch of
her tail, she was gone.

Suddenly everyone stopped and turned
back to face the hill. A crowd of animals
was streaming from the woods: mice, moles,
rats and rabbits tumbled down the hill with
stoats, squirrels, bucks and badgers running

alongside them. A large stag with antlers like oak branches crashed through the corn and Maxwell saw that two small monkeys were riding on its back.

"**MEGAN! MONTY!**" he gasped as the stag stopped and pawed the ground. "What are *you* doing here?"

"We came to help rescue Fern," said Megan. "And we brought a few of our friends with us."

Old Jake the hound stepped forward, flanked by three badgers, two rams and a fierce-looking boar. The young foxhounds stared in amazement.

"And that includes me," said Jake.

Hunter frowned. "I thought hounds were supposed to hate foxes," she growled.

"I used to think like you," replied Jake. "But after Fern fixed my injured paw, I realized that things could be different. Why *can't* a hound be friends with a fox? Why *can't* a farmer dance? Why can't we all hang out together at **The Biscuit and Bone Club**?"

Before Hunter could think of a reply, the
farmer picked himself up from the ground,
caught sight of the crowd of animals staring
at him – and promptly fainted.

CHAPTER TEN

Hide aNd SeeK

"i'VE JUST HAD THE LOVELiEST DREAM,"

murmured the farmer as Monty and Megan

draped him across his horse.

"Hey, Mister Horse," said Chelsea. "Any

chance of a ride?"

"Sure," said the horse. "Jump up."

The chickens clambered on behind the

farmer, and the horse stood up carefully.

"I lost the fox but I didn't care," muttered

the farmer. "Chickens are the **BEST DANCERS iN THE WHOLE WORLD!**"

"*Finally!*" said Cherry.

"*No one* dances *Swan Lake* like a chicken," agreed Chiquita. She looked at Mr B. "Maybe one day you'll dance with us too."

"**YES, YES!**" cried Mr B, clapping his paws and jumping up and down. "We could start our own dog-dancing classes! What do you say, Hunter?"

For a moment, Hunter held Mr B's gaze. Then the foxhound lifted her paw to her ear and mouthed: **CALL ME**.

The rest of the animals looked on as the farmer and his chickens rode off into the sunset. Then Megan leapt up on Monty's shoulders and waved her arms above her head.

"Come on, everyone! This calls for a celebration! Meet you all back at **The Biscuit and Bone Club**!"

Maxwell had never seen so many animals

packed together in such a small space.

Nigel the grass snake was on top of the bar,

showing the squirrels how many biscuits

he could swallow; Megan and Monty were

having a competition to see how many pull-

ups they could do on the stag's antlers and

the mice were lining up in front of a badger

called Kevin who had recently learned to

juggle. He was skilfully throwing the mice

into the air three at a time and those still in

the queue could hardly wait for their turn.

"**WHEEEE!**" they cried. "**ME NEXT!**"

The squirrels at the bar shouted "**TWENTY-**

ONE! TWENTY-TWO!" while Monty dropped

to the floor exhausted. Megan continued

her pull-ups, to the delight of the crowd,

and the noise of rats, rabbits, dogs and foxes
shouting **"PULL! PULL!"** was soon too much for
Maxwell's sensitive ears. He wandered outside
to find somewhere quiet.

Hunter was sitting alone in the shadows beneath the trees.

"Hello, Hunter," said Maxwell. "Is everything all right?"

Hunter stared up at the evening sky. "All this time I've been wary about foxes," she said. "It must have been horrible for Fern to have us chasing her."

"I found it pretty scary myself," said Maxwell.

Hunter looked at him. "You were *such* a rubbish fox."

Maxwell chuckled.

"The thing is," said Hunter, "when I was chasing foxes I had a purpose in life. But what am I going to do now?"

Maxwell listened to the cheers and laughter coming from inside **The Biscuit and Bone Club** and thought how happy everyone sounded. He wanted Hunter to be happy too.

Then he remembered something Mr B had said to him that morning: *The more the merrier.*

"Follow me, Hunter," he said. "I think I might have just the thing for you."

"SO LET ME GET THIS STRAIGHT," said Hunter, leaning against the bar as the animals gathered around her. "All I have to do is stand here with my eyes closed and count to a hundred?"

"Yep," said Maxwell. "And that's when the fun starts. Because then you have to come and *track us down*."

A smile spread across the foxhound's face. **"HM,"** she said. "I think I could be great at this."

"OK, everyone," said Maxwell. "Are we all ready to play?"

"**YES!**" cried the animals. "**PAWS ON EYES! PAWS ON EYES!**"

Hunter looked at Maxwell. "Thanks, kid," she said. Then she turned to the bar and hid her face in her paws.

With squeaks and squeals and woofs and whimpers, the animals ran through the door of **The Biscuit and Bone Club** and soon the only sound came from Hunter, as she counted to a hundred.

Maxwell followed his three friends out into the gathering dusk. Above them the moon rose high above the hill.

"IT'S WEIRD," said Madison, "but I'm so happy I don't feel like punching anyone."

"That is so sweet," said Mr B.

"Something tells me this is going to be the best game of Hide and Seek ever," said Maxwell.

Then, with a last look behind him, he ran with his friends up the narrow woodland track and disappeared into the shadows of the forest.

More MAXWELL MUTT
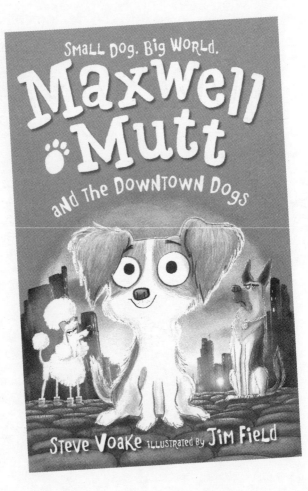 adventures to collect:

SMALL DOG. BIG WORLD.
MaxWell
Mutt
and the DOWNTOWN DOGS

STEVE VOAKE ILLUSTRATED BY JIM FIELD